The Thingamabob

Il Sung Na

One day,
he found the
thingamabob.

He had no idea
what the thingamabob was
or where it came from.

Sometimes,
it didn't do anything at all.

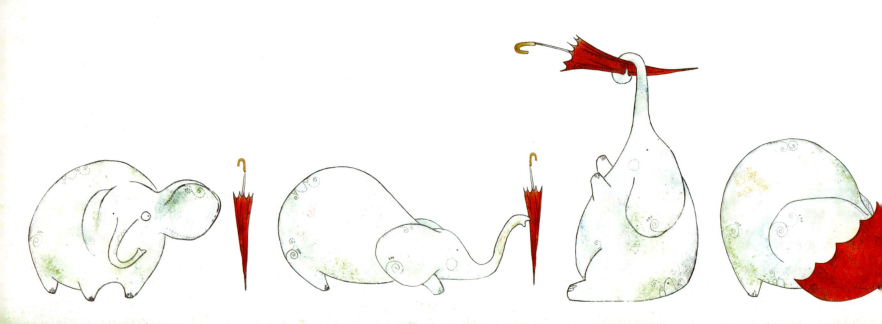

Sometimes,
it gave him a surprise!

He asked his friends...

...but they did not
seem to know.

He thought…
Maybe I can fly with it?

Maybe not.

Maybe I can sail in it?

Maybe not.

Maybe I can hide behind it?

Maybe not.

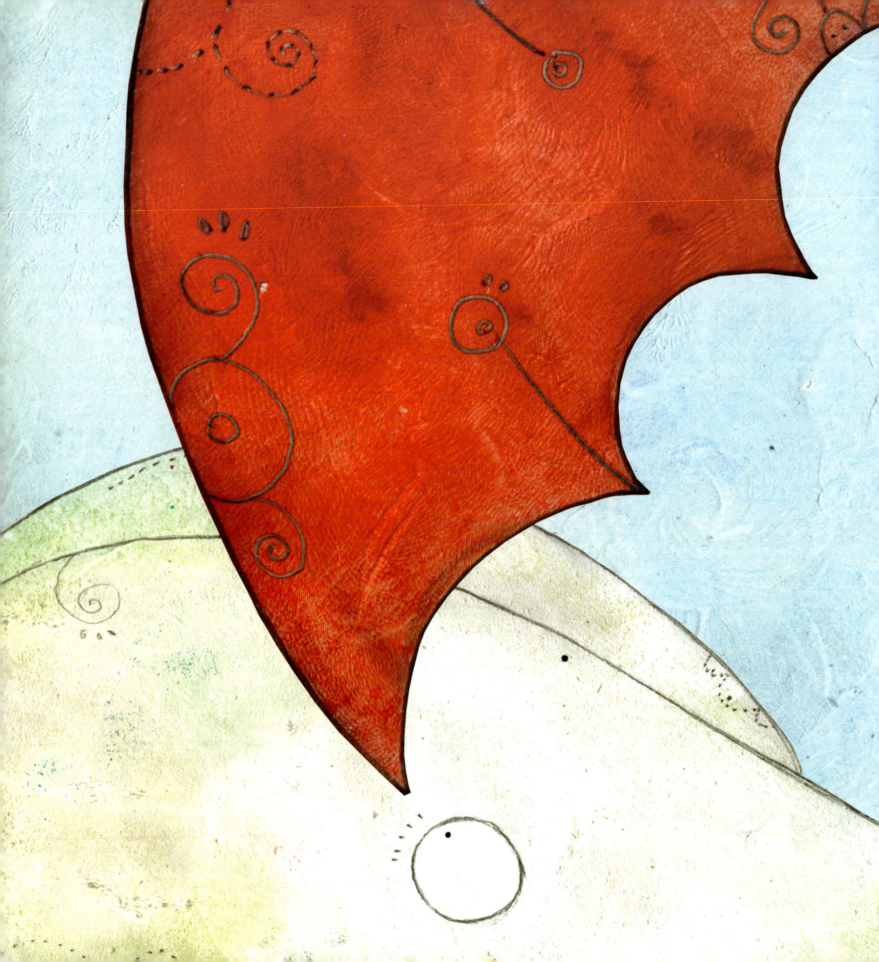

What are you, then!?
he cried.

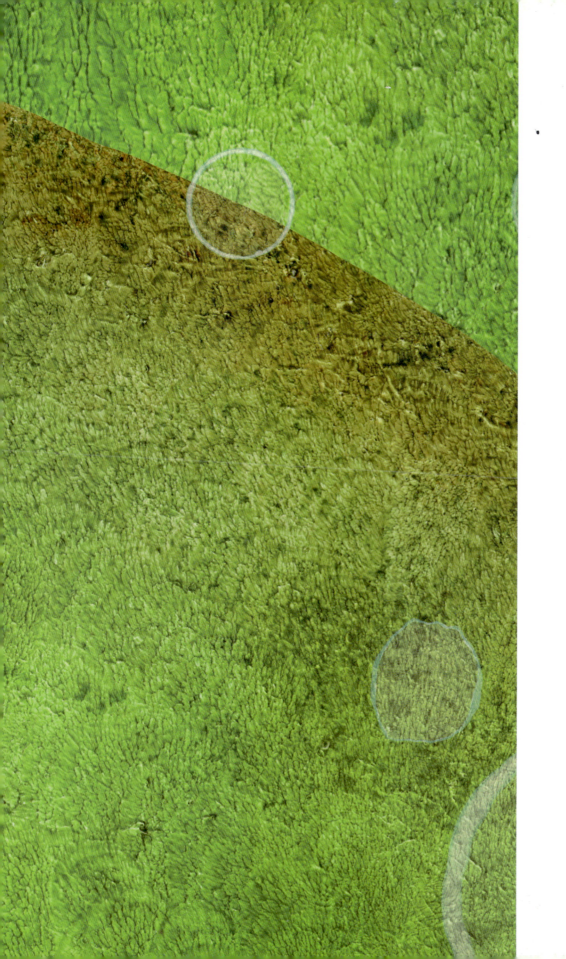

Then
big
drops
of rain
started
to fall.

He did
not want
to get wet.

He did not need
to get wet!

For my nephew Rueben

First published in 2008
by Meadowside Children's Books
185 Fleet Street
London EC4A 2HS
www.meadowsidebooks.com

A CIP catalogue record for this book
is available from the British Library
10 9 8 7 6 5 4 3 2 1
Printed in Indonesia